A Bit of Wee Luck

HOLIDAZE IN SALEM

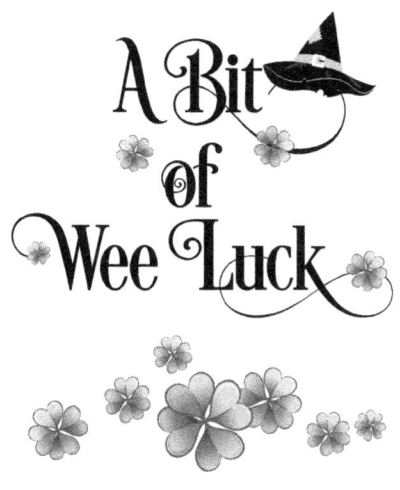

A Bit of Wee Luck

HOLIDAZE IN SALEM

KELLY ELLIOTT

A Bit of Wee Luck
Book 3 Holidaze in Salem © 2023 by Kelly Elliott
Cover Design by: Graphics by Stacy
Interior Design & Formatting by: Elaine York, Allusion Publishing
(http://www.allusionpublishing.com)

This book is a work of fiction. Names, characters, places, and incidents either are products of the author's imagination or are used fictitiously. Any resemblance to actual persons, living or dead, events, or locales is entirely coincidental.

For more information on Kelly and her books, please visit her website www.kellyelliottauthor.com.

Chapter One

Hollie

I stared into Lucas's caramel eyes as he repeated for the fourth time, "A baby?"

Laughing, I nodded. "Can you only say that one word?"

Lucas blinked several times and then shook his head. "We're having a baby?"

"Okay, you added on a few words that time," I deadpanned.

"How?"

I raised my brows and gave him a look.

"No, I know *how*. I thought you were on the pill."

"I am, but nothing is one hundred percent. I've never missed any and I wasn't on any medicine that would affect it, so I guess it's just part of our plan." I drew my lower lip between my teeth before I asked, "Are you upset?"

"Upset?" he asked, surprised by my question. "Hell no, I'm not upset. Hollie, this is amazing. Are you okay with it? I know we never really got around to talking about when we wanted kids."

"Or when we wanted to get married. Which—I think I'd like that to be sooner rather than later. Maybe even here in Ireland! Oh, or Scotland! I've always wanted to go there."

Lucas took my hand in his and kissed the back of it, sending shivers through my entire body. "We can go and do whatever you want while we're over here. And I'll marry you anywhere you want, anytime you want."

I felt my cheeks heat and had to bite the inside of my cheek so I wouldn't say: *Let's run off and get married. To-day.* Instead, I replied, "I know you're working, so I don't expect you to take me all over the place."

He smiled. "With what we keep finding, I might be here longer than I thought. I was going to talk to you about it."

"Well, from what I've seen on the drive in from the airport, I think I'm going to love it here." I spread my arms, taking in the room around us. "I love this little flat! And the town is adorable. It feels like we're in the middle of nowhere, but Dublin isn't that far away. Have you been to the pub across the street yet? It's a real Irish pub, Lucas!"

"I know," he said with a laugh. "I've been there plenty of times. A guy by the name of Benny O'Brien owns it. It was his father's pub, and his before that, and his before that. It's been in the family for a long time. Wait until you eat there. His mother, Sarah, is an amazing cook. Just remember that when they talk they don't make the TH sound."

A bubble of excitement burst in my chest as I said, "Same name as my sister! And I'm starving. Do you think we can grab something to eat there now?"

"Of course. Come on, I'll introduce you to Benny and his family."

Lucas took hold of my hand and helped me off the bed. "You're not too tired? I could run over and get us some food to go."

With a shake of my head, I replied, "I'm tired, but I really want to see the pub, even if it means I can't drink. Let me brush my teeth and change my clothes."

We headed out and started for the pub across the street. It was in a beautiful, old, three-story building with the name *O'Brien's* on a sign out front. It was sandwiched between two other buildings, which both looked to be as old as the pub—though the one on the right was most likely the oldest.

Lucas nodded toward the building. "Benny was raised in the flat above the pub, and now he lives there with his mom and his sister."

"It's so cute. I love the yellow building and the red trim around the windows and doors." I looked up at the numerous plant holders. "They must plant flowers there in the spring."

"They do," Lucas said as he reached for the door to open it. "It's supposed to be beautiful in the spring with all the flowers. There's a story behind it; I'll tell you later."

I smiled, and Lucas opened the door and I stepped inside. My eyes widened as I took in the old pub. Large stone floors made way to the most beautiful wooden bar I'd ever seen. The walls were covered with memorabilia and pictures, as well as some odd items that I was sure held special meaning for the O'Brien family. I glanced up and saw a boot hanging down from the ceiling. I'd loved to know the meaning behind that one. Old photos were scattered behind the bar and throughout the large space. The woodwork was unbelievable. My eyes caught on a beautiful stained-glass window to the left that looked into a small room.

"It's so beautiful," I whispered as we walked farther into the mostly-empty bar. I wasn't sure what I'd been expecting, but I did assume it would be more crowded—especially since it was close to noon.

"Where is everyone?" I whispered.

Lucas sighed. "Folks haven't been coming in much lately. A lot of people have been hit hard in the community and money is tight. Benny's worried he may have to close the pub if things keep going the way they are."

"Oh no! That's terrible. It looks like it's been around for a long time."

"Yeah, it sucks for him and his family," Lucas said with a nod. "It's been open since the late eighteen-hundreds."

A handsome guy in his late 20s or early 30s glanced up from whatever he was reading. He had blondish red hair and eyes so blue I could see them from where we were standing.

"How's it going, Benny?" Lucas asked.

A wide smile grew across his face, and I swore his eyes lit up, especially when he looked at me.

"Grand!"

A younger woman with the same smile as Benny walked out from a back area. It must be his sister Kelley Lucas had mentioned. She looked at Lucas and grinned, but her smile faltered slightly when she saw me. Our eyes met and she quickly grinned again. It was all so fast that if I hadn't been paying attention, I would have missed it.

"Hey, Kelley. How are you today?" Lucas asked.

"I'm suckin' diesel."

My smile faltered and I turned to give Lucas a questioning look. He laughed and said, "Yeah, that one took me a while to figure out. It basically means she's doing good. Or grand. At least, I think that's what it means."

Giggling, I slipped onto a barstool as Lucas introduced me. "Benny, Kelley, this is my fiancée, Hollie Craft."

Benny reached for my hand, his smile growing into a full-on grin. "It's nice to finally meet ya, Hollie. Lucas here has been talking about ya non-stop."

I returned his gesture with a smile of my own. "It's so nice to meet you both."

Kelley shook my hand and asked, "Did ya just arrive?"

Nodding, I replied, "I did and I'm starving. Lucas said you have the best food in town."

Kelley and Benny both beamed. "That we do," Kelley said. "Only because it's me ma who's doing the cooking."

Benny helped his sister into her coat as he said, "We've got Irish stew and bangers and mash."

"Irish stew for me," Lucas quickly said.

"Bangers and Mash?" I asked, one brow raised. "That sounds...interesting and oddly sexual."

Kelley let out a bark of laughter while Benny pointed to me and looked over at Lucas. "I like her."

"So do I," Lucas stated, kissing me on the cheek.

"It's sausage with mashed potatoes and an onion gravy. Side of peas as well," Benny said with a twinkle in his eyes.

My stomach took that moment to growl. "That sounds amazing. I'll have that."

Knocking on the bar, Benny nodded. "I'll go get it for ya."

After he walked into what I was assuming was the kitchen, Kelley let out a sigh and glanced around the pub.

"How are things going?" Lucas asked.

She shrugged. "Hardly anyone showed up last night, which isn't good. We've only been open an hour or so. I'm hoping the lunch crowd will pick up at least. I've got to run; picking up me Ma for an outing."

"See you around, Kelley," Lucas said as she glanced over at me once more.

"It was nice to meet ya."

"You as well," I replied with a smile.

Once Kelley had left, I turned to Lucas. "She doesn't like me."

His eyes went wide. "Why do you say that?"

"It was painfully obvious, Lucas. How could you not see it?"

With a one-shoulder shrug, he said, "I think you're tired and hungry. She likes you; why wouldn't she like you?"

"What did you tell them about me?"

"That you were my fiancée. That we've known each other for as long as I can remember and that you were joining me here."

I lifted a brow. "Did you mention I was a witch?"

He laughed. "As crazy as this may sound, I don't normally go around telling people I'm marrying a witch."

Glancing back at the door, I exhaled. "Well, she either doesn't like me because she likes you, or she doesn't like me for some other reason."

"Hollie, you're being paranoid."

"Alright, here's your lunch. Pint for ya both?" Benny asked.

"I'll take one," Lucas said.

"Just a water for me, please," I replied with a soft smile.

Benny seemed taken aback. "No pint? You're in Ireland, Hollie."

Laughing, I nodded. "And as much as it kills me not to taste the Guinness, I can't."

Screwing his face up in disgust, Benny asked, "Ya don't drink?"

Lucas and I exchanged looks before I gave him a slight nod.

"Hollie's pregnant," he said.

Benny's entire face lit up. "That's wonderful news!"

Lucas's smile was so big I couldn't help but giggle. "I just found out. I mean, Hollie told me a little while ago."

Benny reached for Lucas's hand and shook it. "It's about time we heard some good news in this place."

The door to the pub opened and I turned to see an older man slowly making his way in. He glanced over at the three of us and lifted his hand. "Me pint, Benny, before the missus finds out I'm here."

Benny chuckled and excused himself.

I took a bite of my lunch and let out a soft moan. "Oh my God. I think this is the best food I've ever eaten."

Lucas laughed. "It is good. How are you feeling?"

"Better now that I'm getting some real food. Um, can I have a bite of yours?"

He slid the bowl my way, and I took a few bites and smiled. "That's good too. I have a feeling we'll be eating here often."

Lucas's smile faltered. "I just hope Benny's able to stay open."

"Things are that bad?" I asked in a hushed voice. Benny was engrossed in a conversation with the older gentleman.

"It's not only here; a lot of the older pubs are shutting down. I think the younger generation wants to go to hipper bars or clubs. Which sucks. I love the feel of this place and would kill to have something like it back in Salem."

I nodded and shoveled another bite of food into my mouth. Once I swallowed, I said, "The driver who brought me here from the airport also said a lot of younger people are leaving for places like Dublin."

Lucas nodded. "It's true. These smaller pubs are slowly disappearing."

"What do we do?"

He paused with his fork at his mouth before he slowly lowered it. "*We* do nothing, Hollie. And by that, I mean *you* will not do magick. At all."

I laughed. "Do you think I'm incapable of doing anything without magick now?"

"Yes, I do."

Leaning back, I folded my arms over my chest. "That's mean. And might I add that the few spells I've done have all turned out great!"

"Yeah, after you did another spell to correct the first one you messed up."

My mouth dropped open so I could argue with him, but then I quickly realized he was right. "Touché."

Benny made his way back over to us with a wide smile on his face.

"How's the food?"

"It's amazing!" Lucas and I replied at the same time.

"Ma is good in the kitchen."

I nodded. "I'll say."

A few more people walked into the pub, and I saw the excitement on Benny's face. Lucas dove back into his food while I watched Benny interact with his customers. They were a bit older than me, though not by much. One was in a suit, the other dressed more casually. As they ordered lunch, Benny poured them each a beer. There was clearly an art to pouring a pint of Guinness, Ireland's most popular beer.

After placing the pints down for the two gentlemen, Benny slipped into the kitchen and quickly came back out with two plates and bread. The three of them were soon lost in conversation.

"The one thing you'll notice in Ireland: they love to chat. That's what's so great about the local pubs," Lucas stated.

"Are there any other pubs in this little town?" I asked.

He nodded as he chewed. "Down the road about a mile or so. But Benny's is right here on Main Street, so it's generally considered the local pub."

"What would he do if it closed?"

Turning to look at Benny, Lucas shrugged. "I don't know. I'd hate to think of him having to sell this place since it's been in his family for so long."

I chewed on my lip before I went back to my lunch. My mind started to race, and I made a mental note to call my sister Sarah. She'd know the best spell to put on the pub so we could help out Benny.

Chapter Two

Lucas

After spending nearly all afternoon and night in bed with Hollie, I hated to leave the next morning. But I needed to get to the dig site; I had a lot of catching up to do since I'd been gone most of yesterday. Missing work had been worth it, though. Hollie's surprise...her two surprises...still had me feeling like I was walking on cloud nine.

Leaning down, I kissed Hollie gently on the forehead. "Hollie, I'm leaving for work."

She grunted something that sounded like *I love you* and *have a good day.*

I grabbed an apple and a protein bar and made my way to the dig site. Once I was there, Ryan and Matt caught me up everything that had happened yesterday. They'd found the corner of what appeared to be the stone base of a building. It was another exciting discovery, and I quickly jumped into action.

"You've documented the find in the notebook? And you took photos?" I asked Ryan.

He nodded. "This isn't my first dig site, Lucas."

Smiling, I replied, "I know, sorry."

"How was your time with the missus?" Matt asked. His Irish accent was so thick that I constantly ended up staring at him in confusion because I couldn't understand half the shit he said.

"My missus?"

"Your future wife, your girlfriend."

"Oh! Right. It was great. Took her to O'Brien's for lunch. She loved it. Wanted to go back for dinner as well, but we were busy catching up on lost time."

Both men laughed. "I bet ya were. Will she be staying in Ireland with ya then?" Matt inquired.

I nodded. "She will. She also gave me some great news."

The sound of someone gasping had the three of us looking down at something one of the student archeologists was working on.

"What is that?" Ryan asked, bending down to take a closer look at the ground. Matt and I followed.

"She's pregnant," I said as I narrowed my eyes to look closer at the object slowly emerging from under hundreds of years of dirt.

"No shite." Matt gave me a slap on the back. "Congratulations."

Ryan turned and looked at me, his hand outstretched. "That's great, Lucas. Congratulations."

Smiling, I shook his hand. "Thanks."

"Is that what I think it is?" Matt asked as Ryan and I both turned back to the dig.

I knew they'd both had the same thought I did: that what Lindsay was uncovering appeared to be bone.

Slowly shaking my head, I said, "It's a skull."

Ryan and I looked at each other. "Do you think it's a burial chamber?"

"I think if it was, we'd have found other human remains." Standing, I looked out over the site. "We know they were making leather and possibly blades for weapons. This is clearly the base of a large room." Turning to look at Ryan, I asked, "When does the lidar equipment get here?"

"Tomorrow."

I nodded. "I say we send it up, get some scans, and then decide which way we want to keep going. If this is a compound, we've just stumbled on something much bigger than we thought."

Everyone smiled, and I placed my hand over my pounding heart. "I fucking love working in the field."

By the end of the day, we'd managed to clear away enough to identify what might possibly be a full set of skeletal remains. I'd called Sam Martin, my former college professor and the man who'd invited me on the dig, and had caught him up on our findings over the last two days. To say he was excited was an understatement.

I pulled into the small driveway of the place I was renting and drew in a deep breath. Today had been a hell of a day, and I couldn't wait to turn off my brain and pull Hollie into my arms. I was renting a small apartment in an older building that had been remodeled. It had once been a general store and was now separated into two apartments. Ryan was renting out the other side and was hoping his wife would be able to leave London soon to join him.

"Hollie?" I called out as I tossed my keys into the small bowl that sat on the table in the front entrance.

When I was greeted with silence, I made my way to the bedroom. Hollie had seemed so exhausted earlier this morning. After being a selfish bastard and keeping her up half the night to make love to her, she had only gotten a few hours of sleep before she'd woken up and run to the bathroom to threw up.

I frowned when I found the bedroom empty as well. Turning, I headed to the kitchen where I found an apple pie sitting on the table.

"Apple pie? Is she missing home already?"

I peeked out into the small area out back, but she wasn't there, so I called her. She picked up after one ring.

"Hey! Are you home?" she asked.

"I am, where are you?"

I could hear someone else taking in the background.

"I'm over at O'Brien's. I was dying to try another one of Benny's dishes, so I came here for lunch."

"And you're still there?"

"Yep!"

"What in the hell have you been doing there all this time?"

Hollie laughed. "Well, I met Benny's mother, Sarah, though he calls her Ma. Anyway, she decided she needed to teach me how to make a few Irish dishes. After that, she took me to Dunnes, which is a grocery store, though they call it the market. I picked up some stuff for us and I told Sarah I would make her an apple pie—so don't eat that apple pie in the kitchen."

"Okay, so why are you back over at O'Brien's?"

"I wanted to know more about the pub, so I walked over to talk to Benny. You weren't lying when you said the Irish like to talk. I've been chatting with this older man for two hours! His name is Willy, and I'm pretty sure I know his entire life story."

It was my turn to laugh. "Do you need me to come over and save you?"

"If you don't mind, that would be great!"

With a chuckle, I replied, "I'm on my way."

The moment I walked in, I spied Hollie at a table with three older men. She clearly had them all in a trance, and I highly doubted she'd used magick to do it. She was saying something, and they were all ears.

"I find it hard to believe she doesn't have any Irish in her. She can talk your ear off," Benny said as he slid a pint toward me. I laughed and picked it up before putting some money down for it. Benny had refused to take my money at first, but I told him I would stop coming in after work if he didn't start taking it, so he'd reluctantly agreed.

"Can't say I'm surprised to see Hollie here," I said.

Benny chuckled. "She got along famously with me Ma. They were in the kitchen for a bit then went to the market."

"That's what Hollie said. She made an apple pie."

He let out a roar of laughter that made everyone at Hollie's table glance over. Hollie smiled from ear to ear when she saw me, and I felt my heart skip a beat in my chest. I wondered how long that feeling of losing my breath at the sight of her would last.

Hollie excused herself and made her way over to me. After kissing me on the cheek, she looked at Benny. "Thank you so much for letting me hang with you today."

He nodded, but I could tell he was confused before he finally realized what she meant. "It was me pleasure. Stop by anytime ya want."

When I saw the way Hollie lit up, I knew Benny had just made a terrible error.

Chapter Three

Hollie

Over the next two days, I spent nearly all of my time at O'Brien's getting to know Benny, his mother, and Kelley. I'd laughed so much my sides ached. I'd also learned how to make a few traditional Irish dishes and had showed Sarah and Kelley the secrets to my apple pie recipe. According to Kelley, the apple pie I'd brought over for her mother was gone within a quarter of an hour.

On my fourth day in Ireland, I opened the door to our flat, kicked off my boots, and hung up my coat. I wasn't sure how Lucas was working in this cold weather. It was freezing and raining most of the time. Even though a majority of the dig site was covered with tents, they were under a tight deadline to discover exactly what the site was in order to determine if they'd need to build a tunnel through the area.

Flopping down onto the sofa, I let out a yawn. It didn't seem to take much to tire me out these days. No doubt because I was making a baby. I smiled as I placed my hand on my stomach and then dropped my head back.

I replayed the conversations I'd had with the O'Brien's over the last few days in my mind. Sarah was beyond upset at the idea that the family pub might have to close its doors. Kelley was stressed about what they were all going to do if it did. The more I got to know her, the more I realized I had pegged her totally wrong when I'd first met her. I'd thought she might have had a thing for Lucas, but it was far from the truth. I could see us becoming close friends if we stayed in Ireland for a longer length of time.

My mind drifted to a recent conversation I'd had with Benny. I could tell he was simply lost about what to do with the pub. Chewing on my lip, I picked up my phone and asked, "Hey Siri, what time is it in Boston, Massachusetts?"

When she replied that it was half past nine at night, I smiled and hit my sister Sarah's number.

"Hey! Still loving Ireland?"

"I am! It rains every day, though. Not all day, but enough to be thankful for our weather in Salem."

"Ugh, if you say so. It currently snowing, and I'm so cold my nipples could cut glass."

I couldn't help but laugh.

"How's the dig going for Lucas?"

"Great! They've found a lot of skeletons, and from his happy chatter, I'm guessing that's a good thing. I honestly start to tune out what he talks about work because...well... it's boring."

Sarah laughed.

I'd been so busy settling in I had meant to call Sarah sooner to ask about a spell. "I have made a few friends, though. There's an Irish pub right across the street from the flat we're renting. It's been in their family for years. The son runs it now; his name is Benny. His mother, Sarah, does most of the cooking and his sister Kelley helps."

"I think I'm rather fond of the mother's name."

Giggling, I replied, "I knew you would be. Listen...Sarah...I need your help."

There was a moment of silence before she said, "No."

"You don't even know what I'm going to ask you."

"I know, trust me. You forget, Hollie, that I'm also a witch, and although I can't read minds like you can, I already know what you're going to ask. You want help with a spell."

My shoulders slumped. "Fine, that was what I was going to ask you to help with. But this is important, Sarah. Benny's going to lose his pub if I don't do anything. I only need a small little spell to bring him some good fortune."

"There's no such thing as a small little spell with you, darling sister. With you it's...well, I don't even know what it's like. How you manage to mess up every spell is beyond me."

"It's because you won't help, and may I remind you...I'm new at this!"

"I've already helped you get yourself out of trouble with two spells that have gone wrong, and you've only just accepted your gift. You need to stop jumping in head first with the spells."

I let out a dramatic sigh. Then I turned to plan b. Whining.

"Sarah, pleeeeease. I really want to help this family. I like them so much, and they've been so kind to Lucas. I'll do anything you say if you'll just please help me with a spell."

"Anything?"

My felt my breath catch. Holy hell, if I'd known that was all it would take to get her to help me, I'd have offered it up before. "Yes! Anything!"

She paused for a moment. "I don't know."

"*Any. Thing*," I said.

"Mom is going to kill me!"

I let out a little scream as I stood up. "I love you so much, Sarah! Now, what do I need to do?"

23

"I'll tell you how to set up the altar table, but you'll have to come up with the spell. It has to come from you to make it more potent."

I nodded. "Okay, I can do that. I mean, how hard is it to come up with a spell?"

She huffed on the other end of the phone. "You have to promise me one thing. If something goes wrong, you'll figure out how to fix it."

I chewed nervously on my lip once again, then I smiled. If something went wrong, I'd simply call my best friend Kristin. She'd help me. She was new to this whole witch thing, but I knew we'd be able to figure it out together.

"I'm perfectly fine with that since nothing's going to happen."

When Sarah replied, I could hear a smile in her voice. "If you say so."

I needed to move quickly since Lucas would be home soon. I cleared off the table, got a candle, and set my cinnamon sticks down. I didn't have a smudge stick, but that was probably a good thing. I placed the incense down over the cinnamon, and sprinkled out some dried dandelion leaf and basil. Sarah had said I'd need some verbena, but I wasn't able to find any at the market, so I'd grabbed jasmine instead.

I lit the candle, put a circle of freshly ground cinnamon around it, then lit the incense.

I took a piece of lace, laid it directly in front of me, and placed some cash on it. Then I set down a four-leaf clover that I'd picked up at the airport. I wasn't really sure if it was real or not, but I wasn't going to second guess it. I was just glad I'd foreseen its importance.

I'd written my spell in less than five minutes and couldn't wait to brag to Sarah about it. The next thing I needed was a hair clip, which would stand in place of a money clip. The very last item had been a bit tricky, but Sarah had insisted that I needed a piece of Benny's hair. So I'd begged him to show me how to pour a pint of Guinness, and while his back was turned, I'd reached up and pulled out a few strands. He'd let out a scream so girlish I'd peed myself laughing. I'd just told him he had something in his hair and had pocketed the strands.

Picking up the incense, I drew in a deep breath as I moved it around the table.

I picked up the pieces of Benny's hair and then said my spell.

"A fourth leaf cloverA wad of cashA money clip to store it fastLight it on fire and listen to me, all good will and fortune go unto thee.

Bring Benny loads of luck

And please don't let this spell suck.

Good fortune to fall on my Irish friend

Hang on tight, Benny

This spell will break the trend."

I dropped his hair into the fire then sprinkled the herbs over the flame. The flame grew larger and the fire crackled, which only made me smile.

"I did it! I did a spell all on my own! Take that Sarah!"

An hour later, after I'd cleaned up all the evidence of my spell doing, Lucas walked in looking exhausted and cold.

"You must be freezing!" I said as I rushed over to him.

"I am. I want out of these clothes and to eat a hot meal."

After helping him remove his coat and boots, I quickly headed into the bathroom and turned on the shower. Lucas stripped out of his clothes and stepped in before it was even very hot.

"It's not ready yet!" I stated.

"Anything's better than cold rain."

I smiled and sat on the edge of the tub while he showered. "Would you like me to make you something? I have sandwich stuff."

"Would you mind if we went to the pub, Hollie? A bowl of Irish stew sounds so damn good right about now."

My stomach twisted slightly with nerves, but I ignored it. "That sounds amazing. I'll grab you some clothes and set them on the counter."

I placed Lucas's clothes on the counter then made my way over to the front window to look out at the pub. Frowning, I didn't really notice many people coming or going. As a matter of fact, I didn't see anyone go in the entire time I stood there and watched.

"Damn it."

"What's wrong?" Lucas asked as he walked up and pulled me to him.

"Nothing. I was thinking about something I forgot to tell Mindy about a party we have coming up."

Ugh, that lie came quicker than I would have liked.

"You ready to head across the street?" Lucas asked before he leaned down and kissed me gently on the mouth. "By the way, you look beautiful today. There's a glow about you."

Wrapping my arms around his neck, I smiled as I gazed up into his caramel eyes. "Maybe it's because I'm with you."

He grinned. "Maybe, but I think it has more to do with you being pregnant."

"That too!" I stated. "You ready to go eat?"

"I am so ready!"

Chapter Four

Lucas

It had been nearly two weeks since Hollie had arrived in Ireland. We'd shut the dig site down for a much-needed long weekend, and Hollie and I drove over to the Cliffs of Moher. It was one of the most beautiful places I'd ever seen. The vertical drop made both of us dizzy, but the sounds of the ocean crashing against the limestone cliff was almost mystical. I saw the awe on Hollie's face as she stood there and stared out over the water. Wrapping her arms around her, she almost looked as if she was returning to a treasured spot. I had to practically drag her back to the car to get her out of the cold.

"I cannot wait to have some shepherd's pie," Hollie said later that night as we made our way across the street and toward O'Brien's. She intertwined her fingers with mine, giving my hand a squeeze.

"You're going to turn into a shepherd's pie if that's all you keep eating, Hollie."

She laughed then walked into the pub. Benny was behind the bar, whistling away as if he hadn't a care in the world.

"Benny seems to be in a good mood," I stated as Hollie's face lit up.

"Hey Benny!" I called out, drawing his attention away from wiping down the bar and over to us. I pulled a barstool out for Hollie, and she climbed on. Benny grinned as he poured me a pint and made an ice water for Hollie.

Looking a little too hopeful, Hollie asked, "What has you in such a good mood?"

That was when Benny blushed. I knew that look. It was the look of man who'd spent some time in a woman's bed and had thoroughly enjoyed it.

"You're not going to believe what happened to me," he stated.

Hollie nearly bounced in her seat with anticipation. "What? Tell us!"

Benny laughed and said, "Last night at closing, Casey Storm came in looking for me."

"Who's Casey Storm?" I asked.

"Casey Storm is the girl I swore I was going to marry. She ended up marrying some rich bastard from London and moved away. She's back now and divorced."

"And that's a good thing?" Hollie asked, stretching out the 'ing.'

If Benny had blushed before, now he was nearly as red as a tomato. "Probably not something to talk about in front of ya, Hollie."

Hollie looked confused. "Why not?"

Before he could explain, she made an eeep sound and slid off the stool. "Wait, don't say a word until I get back! I have to pee!"

She made a beeline for the lady's bathroom. The moment she was gone, I looked back at Benny.

"Casey came walking in here last night with one thing on her mind."

I chuckled. "What was that?"

"Fucking."

With his thick Irish accent, I wasn't quite sure what I'd just heard. "I'm sorry?"

"She walked right up to me after the last person left. Said she was no longer with her husband, and she needed a good fuck. It was the best night of me fucking life. She was like an animal. I've never fucked on the bar, but I plan on doing it a lot more."

I glanced down at the bar and curled my lip.

"Don't worry, it was down there, and I cleaned it twice."

My brows rose. "Just so I know for the future, where else did you two have sex?"

He shook his head. "We didn't have sex, Lucas. We fucked. Like rabbits. Oh, that table over there, I bent her over and took her from behind."

I had made a mental note to tell Hollie not to sit at the left end of the bar or at the table in the back-left corner.

"She's coming over to me place later tonight. This time I plan on fucking her in me bed."

I was beginning to wonder if I should keep track of how many times Benny had said fuck.

"It was the best fucking night of me life."

Nodding, I replied, "You mentioned that."

Hollie walked up and smiled as she slid onto the bar-stool.

"What did I miss?" she asked, looking between me and Benny.

I cleared my throat and said, "Apparently, Benny and his ex had a bit of fun in the pub last night. At that end of the bar—" I pointed to it—"and then again at that table over there in the corner."

Leaning in, I said, "Don't ever sit at either spot. They had sex there."

"Sex?" Hollie practically shouted. "That was it? Just sex?"

Benny's eyes went wide. "Just sex? It was the best night of me life. She was…"

He let his words trail off.

"She was what? Rich? Offered to become partners with you?" Hollie asked as Benny and I both looked at her with a confused expression.

"No," Benny replied. "We just fucked."

I was pretty sure he was up to seven fucks.

"Why would you think she'd become partners with him?" I asked Hollie.

She shrugged. "I don't know. He seemed so happy. I wasn't aware that sex could make you so happy the day after."

Benny smiled. "Hell yeah, it was the kind of sex that…"

"Okay, I think we get it." I held up my hand to keep him from going on. "How about two orders of shepherd's pie if you still have some."

"I do!" Benny turned and headed to the kitchen.

I looked at Hollie and let out a chuckle. "I'm going to guess it's been a while since our boy Benny had sex—or this Casey girl was the one who got away."

Hollie giggled. "I'd say both."

After bringing us our food, Benny went down to the other end of the bar to help the two men who'd just walked in and sat down. Poor bastards had no idea what Benny had done on that bar less than twenty-four hours ago.

An older couple sat down next to Hollie and the four of us soon fell into a conversation. They had spent some time in America and wanted to know all about Salem and the history of the witches. Little did they know, they were talking to an actual witch.

After they left, I pulled out some money to pay for our meal and Benny walked back over.

"I got the strangest email a few minutes ago," he said.

"What was it?" Hollie asked.

"Some lady wants to pay me nearly five-hundred euros for a picture of me feet."

"What?" I asked on a burst of laughter. "Are you sure it was your feet and not your..."

"Lucas!" Hollie hit me playfully on the chest.

"No, it was me feet. Apparently, some people are into that."

Looking confused, Hollie asked, "Into it how exactly?"

Benny shrugged. "It's called podophilia."

Hollie's mouth fell open and it took everything I had in me not to laugh. "You've never heard of people having a foot fetish before?" I asked.

"Of course I have," she said, once she remembered how to talk. "But to pay someone for pictures of their feet? She doesn't even want to see your feet in person?"

"Oh, she does. She offered a thousand euros to be able to come and touch them. I declined. That seems a tad bit too much."

"You think?" Hollie stated. "That's just weird."

Benny shrugged. "I'll send the pictures, though."

"What?" Hollie and I both said.

"Hey, five-hundred euros is a lot of money. I'll take it any way I can get it."

I shook my head while Hollie appeared to gag.

The bell on the door rang and the three of us looked over to see a group of women around our age entering the pub.

"Good evening, ladies," Benny called out. The dark-haired girl in the front glanced back at the others who appeared to encourage her to step forward.

She cleared her throat and made her way over to the bar. She was far enough away that I'm sure she thought her conversation was private, but it was far from it. Especially with Hollie leaning in her direction so she could listen.

"How may I help ya?" Benny asked.

The young woman looked embarrassed as she said, "We're friends with Casey and she, um, well, she told us how lovely your, um, your pub was. We were wondering if we could hold our weekly book club meetings here. We'll pay ya, of course."

Hollie nearly fell out of her chair. I had to grab her to keep her from falling to the ground.

"What happened?" I asked.

Hollie turned to me. "What is she hoping to get out of this book club?"

I couldn't help but chuckle. "I don't think anything like that."

Hollie raised a single brow and then focused back on Benny and the young woman.

"Ya want to have your book club here?" he asked. "In the pub?"

The woman nodded. "Yes. And we'd pay ya since our group is large."

I could see Benny's mind going a mile a minute. "What day of the week is your book club?"

"Mondays."

It was the slowest day of the week at the pub, so I knew Benny would agree.

"You're more than welcome to hold your meeting here. But ya don't have to be paying. Just buy a few pints and we'll call it good."

The young woman blushed. "That's very kind of ya. Casey speaks *fondly* of ya."

"Does she?" Benny asked, causing the young girl to blush even more.

"Yes, she does. I was wondering if you're ever free to go out to dinner or maybe even breakfast."

Benny's brows rose. "Are ya asking me out?"

She nodded.

"I can do breakfast, if it's early enough, but I should tell ya, I'm dating Casey right now."

It was my turn to raise my brows. According to Benny earlier, they'd only been fucking.

Handing him what looked to be a business card, the woman said, "Me name is Karen."

Benny picked up the card. "Nice to meet ya, Karen. I'll call ya then."

A brilliant smile appeared on her face. She walked past us and started to giggle with the other girls as they all left. Spinning in her seat, Hollie looked at Benny, then back to the door. She looked utterly confused, then panicked. When she looked at me, my stomach dropped, and I instantly knew what she was up to.

"What did you do, Hollie?" I asked.

"What? I don't know what you mean."

Leaning in closer to her, I whispered, "You put a spell on him, didn't you?"

She dug her upper teeth into her lower lip as she blinked rapidly and looked everywhere but at me.

"Hollie!" I whispered-shouted. "I told you not to put a spell on him."

"I needed to do something to help him, and when I talked to Sarah about it, she said I had to make up the spell myself. It was a wealth spell!"

I closed my eyes and groaned. "A wealth of what? Sex?"

"No! Of course not!" she spat back at me. "What is wrong with me? Why do my spells keep turning out all wrong?"

I closed my eyes once again and counted to ten. When I opened them, Hollie was watching Benny.

"Why do you think he's smiling down at his phone like that?" she asked.

"God only knows." I sighed. "Hollie, we can't reverse the spell, because if we even attempt to tell Benny you're a witch he'll never let us in here again!"

"We don't have to reverse it. Let me call Sarah and find out what went wrong."

"What went wrong?" I whispered-shouted again. "You did yet another spell!"

She shot me a dirty look before she got up and headed out of the pub. When Benny walked over, he was shaking his head.

"I've died and gone to heaven. Casey wants to have a threesome with Karen."

I was positive my jaw hit the bar. Maybe I should pretend that Hollie never put a spell on Benny. It seemed to be working out fine for him.

"Are you going to?"

He looked at me with an expression of pure shock. "How could ya even ask that? Hell yes, I'm going to."

What in the hell kind of spell did Hollie put on Benny?

Chapter Five

Hollie

Pacing the living room in our flat, I went over the spell in my head.

"What exactly did it say?" Lucas asked.

"I wrote it down, hold on." I rushed over to my notebook and pulled it out. "Here, this is it."

He read the spell on the paper.

A fourth leaf cloverA wad of cashA money clip to store it fastLight it on fire and listen to me, all good will and fortune go unto thee.
Bring Benny loads of luck
And please don't let this spell suck.
Good fortune to fall on my Irish friend
Hang on tight, Benny
This spell will break the trend.

He glanced up at me. "Please don't let this spell suck?"

Shrugging, I replied, "I mean it couldn't hurt to add it, right?"

Lucas sighed then looked back at the spell. "I mean, you do say good fortune."

Chewing on my lip, I asked, "You don't think it's just a coincidence?"

He raised his brows. "Pictures of his feet? A threesome?"

"Wait...a threesome? When did that happen?"

He pushed his hand through his hair. "Karen and Casey—I guess they want to have a bit of fun with Benny."

I felt myself blush. "A bit of fun?"

He shrugged.

"Damn it!" I started to pace again. "This wasn't how it was supposed to go. He was supposed to come into some cash. Not sex."

"Did you talk to Sarah?"

I shook my head. "No. I'm afraid to call her because then she's going to give me a lecture about how I shouldn't be putting spells on people."

"Does it make a difference that you used his hair?"

"I'm sure it made it more potent."

We both sighed right before my phone rang.

"Oh God," I said as I looked at it. "It's Sarah. She knows!"

"Answer it, she might be able to help us."

I swiped my finger across the phone and said in a voice that was way too happy, "Hey Sis! How's it going?"

There was a slight pause before she groaned. "Oh no."

My eyes darted up to Lucas who was attempting—and failing—to hide a smile.

"What do you mean, *oh no*?" I asked.

"You did the spell, didn't you?"

I swallowed hard. "I did, and I have to say, it was a brilliant spell...but the outcome wasn't so brilliant. Well, Benny might not think so since he's getting a threesome out of it."

Sarah choked and then sputtered something into the phone that I couldn't understand.

"Wait, I thought the guy needed money...not sex."

"He does! I think it was my wording."

Lucas walked up and leaned down toward my phone. "She said she wished for good fortune to fall on him."

"Okay, well, that isn't so bad. Were you thinking about sex at the time?" Sarah asked.

"Why in the hell would I be thinking about sex while putting a spell on the guy who owns the local pub?"

Lucas looked at me with an odd expression. I shook my head and whispered, "I wasn't thinking about sex!"

"Okay, well...has he had any good fortune besides sex?" Sarah asked.

"Someone did email him about pictures of his feet," I said. "They're going to pay him. Then a group of women came in and asked to hold a group meeting at his pub. Turns out they heard about it from his ex, who I had guess an amazing night of sex with him there last night."

"I'm going to regret asking this, but where does the threesome come into play? Please tell me it's not with the foot-fetish person."

I giggled. "Benny's ex came back into town and went to see him at the pub. They had a steamy night, apparently."

Lucas added, "And this Casey girl told some friends about said steamy night, and now they want to have their weekly book club meeting at the pub."

"Yes!" I broke in. "And Casey and Karen are the ones who want to have the threesome with Benny."

Looking at Lucas, I asked, "Is he going to? I thought he really liked Casey."

"Yes, he's going to," Lucas replied as if it I should have already known the answer.

I rolled my eyes.

Sarah broke into our side conversation. "Read me the spell."

For the next few minutes, I went over the spell, how I laid out the altar table, and even how I got a piece of his hair.

"I did stop and grab a snack in-between—eating for two, you know."

Lucas looked at me and I froze. We hadn't told anyone back home that I was pregnant yet.

"What did you just say?" Sarah asked.

"Nothing."

"Oh my God...I knew it! I knew it! I even told Lucy I felt like the coven was going to be getting a new witch."

"What?" Lucas and I both said at the same time.

"Hollie, you're pregnant and the baby probably has your powers. And that makes any spell you do while pregnant that much more powerful. It explains everything now. This Benny guy is going to have double the good fortune fall upon him. Let's just hope some of it comes in the form of cash."

Lucas and I stared at one another.

"By the way—" Sarah paused, then screamed, "You're pregnant! Oh my God, this is such amazing news! Congratulations to both of you!"

Smiling, I placed my hand over my stomach and said, "Thank you. We haven't told anyone back home yet. I'm not that far along, so I'm sure you understand."

"Of course! I promise I won't say a word. Mom might sense it, though, like I did. If she asks, I'll act like I know nothing."

"Thank you, Sarah."

Lucas pinched the bridge of his nose. "So wait, you're telling me that our child is most likely a witch?"

"Yep," Sarah said with a giggle.

"Is this common?" I asked.

"I'm not entirely sure how it all works. I do know that there are some children born of witches who don't have any gifts. It's rare, though."

I slowly shook my head. "Okay, well, that's something we'll have to deal with later. In the meantime, if I do a spell, it's more than likely that the little one's powers will mix with mine?"

"Yes. Think about it, Hollie. She's part of you right now."

"Or he!" Lucas interjected.

Chuckling, Sarah replied, "Or he. Even though they're most likely the size of a peanut, they could very well have the same gifts as you. That makes your powers that much stronger."

"Like when you use certain smudge sticks."

Sarah cleared her throat. "Um, yeah, I guess you could say that. I do think it's a bit different here."

I rolled my eyes, even though she couldn't see me. "Of course I realize that. Well, crap. Maybe I need to lay off the spells."

"Yes!" Sarah and Lucas said in unison.

Snarling my lip at the phone and then at Lucas, I huffed, "It could have been worse."

"Yeah, he could be falling and breaking a leg or ending up in the hospital after being hit by a car."

I brought my hand to my hip. "I'm never going to live that down, am I?"

"Well, you did put a hex on him," Sarah added with humor in her voice.

"It was a mistake!" I nearly shouted. "I didn't even realize I was a witch at the time."

Lucas took the phone from my hand. "Is there anything we can do to lessen the spell on Benny without him knowing Hollie's a witch?"

"I can see why you wouldn't want him to know. Let me talk to Lucy and my mother. I'll keep out the fact that you're expecting. They might have an idea to slow down the...uh... good fortune."

Lucas and I both looked at each other. "I'm sure he's enjoying the attention," I said, "but the idea was to save his pub, not overwork his todger."

"I'm sorry...his what?" Sarah asked.

Laughing, I said, "Todger. It's a slang word for penis."

Lucas closed his eyes and slightly shook his head. "Do I even want to know where you learned that?"

Patting him on the chest, I replied, "It's all good. I read it in Prince Harry's biography."

Lucas opened his mouth to say something then quickly shut it.

Sarah cleared her throat. "And this is where we say goodbye. I'll be in touch. In the meantime, Hollie, no spells!"

I rolled my eyes. "Fine, no spells."

Chapter Six

Lucas

I stepped into the pub and cautiously looked around. With the dig site again shut down for a few days, Hollie and I had time to explore Ireland, and it also meant we were spending more time at the pub.

"Lucas!" Benny called out as he made his way over to me. "Pint?"

"Please." I slipped onto a barstool. There were only three open spots at the bar, which wasn't normal for a midweek day, even at lunch time.

"What's going on? The place is pretty full."

Benny looked around and smiled. "Where do I start?"

I smiled as watched him expertly pour me a Guinness. He put it on the counter and slid it my way, not even spilling an ounce of the foam.

"Are you giving away free beer or something?"

His head fell back, and he let out a loud laugh. "No! It seems that word has gotten out that me ma's food is some of the most authentic in Ireland. These lads are in from Dublin.

They were attending a conference and one of the wee girls in the book club told her husband about me ma's Irish stew. He told someone else who works for the company all these Americans work for. They all decided to come to O'Brien's to try out the food!"

"That's wonderful, Benny."

He smiled, though it didn't reach his eyes. "It's a good start, but I'm afraid I'm gonna need a lot more of this if I hope to keep the pub open."

I cleared my throat and looked to make sure no one was listening. "Casey and Karen?"

He blushed. "Christ almighty, Lucas. Casey was wanting to fulfill a fantasy of watching me with another woman. I was all for it at first, but then got to thinking. I really like Casey and ya know, I don't want to risk losing her again."

I nodded. If Hollie ever approached me with a similar request, I wouldn't know what to think. But I knew I wouldn't want to do it, because I loved Hollie and wouldn't want to risk losing her.

"I get it, I'd feel the same way," I stated.

"Yes! But she begged me, Lucas. Said it would only be the one time."

"So you did it?" I asked, taking another look around.

He rubbed at the back of his neck with his hand. "I did. Was the most erotic night of me life. Casey has been coming over to me house every night since. I'm fucking exhausted from all the sex."

I laughed. "So things are moving along with Casey?"

He nodded.

The bell above the door rang and a well-dressed guy around the same age as Benny walked in. Benny tapped on the bar in front of me. "Food?"

"No," I said. "I really just came to see how you were doing since I hadn't spoken to you in a few days."

He winked then said, "I'll be right back."

Benny welcomed the guy and asked if he wanted a pint. The guy sat down, looked around the pub, and caught my eye. He nodded, so I nodded back and added a smile.

After pouring the guy a pint, Benny spoke with him for a few moments before heading back down the bar to check on everyone. Kelley came out from the back with a tray full of food. I watched her make the trip a few more times before Benny brought a plate out for the guy at the bar.

"Who's the serious looking gent?" I asked, jerking my head in the direction of the well-dressed guy who clearly looked out of place in the pub. He was wearing a suit that looked expensive.

Benny shrugged. "He's in from Dublin. For business, he said."

"Benny!" Kelley shouted. "Call!"

"I'll be right back," he said before heading over to the phone. When his eyes went wide, I nearly groaned. What could it be now? He spoke into the receiver for a few more minutes while I finished my drink.

I couldn't help but notice that the guy in the suit was looking around the bar. He was definitely checking it out. What if he was a developer who'd caught wind that Benny might have to shut the pub down? He could be looking to build some apartment building or something. That would really suck.

"You're not going to believe who just called," Benny said as he joined me again.

"You'd be surprised," I said and Benny gave me a funny look. "Who was it?"

"A movie director. He's looking for an authentic pub to film a few scenes in. They're filming down the road, and he asked some locals if there was a pub nearby. They mentioned O'Brien's and now he wants to stop by and check out the place. If they end up using it, he'll pay us a large amount to rent the pub out for a week, maybe two!"

"Benny, that's amazing," I said as I watched a little bit of the stress lift away from his face.

"It won't get me completely out of debt, but it'll help pay off a lot of it."

"When's he stopping by?"

Benny looked over at the clock on the wall. "Thirty minutes."

He pronounced it as *tirty*, and it took me a second to figure out he meant *thirty*. Sometimes it was still jarring to hear how the Irish didn't pronounce the TH sound.

"If they rent the pub out, will you have to turn away customers?"

"He said he didn't think we would as they'd do a lot of the filming at night. They might shoot a few scenes during the day and if there are customers here, then it'll be better for the shot. They won't have to worry about extras, as long as everyone is willing to sign a waiver."

"I hope it all works out for you."

On my right, I heard a male voice call out, "Thank ya for the pint!" But it sounded more like, *tank ya.*

Benny held up his hand to the man in the suit and called back, "Any time, lad!"

When Benny turned to face me again, I could see the happiness on his face. "Things might finally be changing for me, Lucas. And for the good!"

Hollie stared at me with a shocked expression on her face. "A movie director?"

I laughed. "Yes. And the place was packed for lunch today. Apparently, word's getting out about Benny's mother's cooking."

Hollie sighed. "She's the best cook. Her potato soup is the best I've ever had. She makes everything taste like heaven. I swear she deconstructed my apple pie and made it her own way. It was the best apple pie I've ever had!"

Laughing once again, I pushed my hand through my hair. "I wonder if we should just leave the spell alone. I mean, does it have a time limit?"

Grinning, Hollie said, "I didn't put one in the spell, so I'm not sure. I don't think so. Maybe the spell interprets good fortune and once it feels like Benny has hit it, it stops."

I stared at her. "You don't really think it works that way, do you?"

She shook her head. "No, but it's wishful thinking. I really don't want to mess things up for Benny. So what if he gets a bit of sex here and there and request for pictures of his feet? What's the harm in it?"

I was pretty sure my mouth fell into my lap. "What if Benny and Casey get together and women keep throwing themselves at Benny? I mean, Casey wanted to share him once, but it doesn't mean she'd want to do it again."

Hollie gasped. "So he *did* have the threesome!"

"He did, though it sounds like it was a one and done kind of thing."

Her brows rose. "Casey wants a relationship with Benny?"

I shrugged. "Sounds like it."

Folding her arms over her chest, Hollie asked, "Then why ask to have a threesome with your friend and the guy you're interested in?"

"According to Benny, it was a fantasy of hers."

"Whatever floats your boat, I guess. The good news is that this movie thing sounds like it might help Benny out."

"He said it would pay some of his bills, but it doesn't sound like it will bail him all the way out."

Sighing, Hollie sat down on the sofa. "I wish we could do more."

"*We*...already did enough. Let's see how things turn out. In the meantime, you keep your spells to yourself."

Hollie crossed her heart with her finger then smiled at me. "I've been thinking... Can we take a trip over to Scotland?"

"Of course we can. Anywhere you want to go in particular?"

Smiling, she got up and walked over to where I was sitting on the sofa. She sat down on my lap and dug her teeth into her bottom lip.

"Why do I feel like you have a plan brewing in that mind of yours?" I asked.

"Because I do—which shows how well you know me. I checked into getting married here in Ireland and it's going to take at least three months. We'd need to have our parents send us our birth certificates and it would be a pain. But in Scotland we can get married with no wait, no resident restrictions or anything."

I raised my brows. "Seriously?"

She nodded her head. "Yes! We can have the ceremony when we get back to Salem, but I really want to get married before I get too far along."

"Hollie, I don't need a reason to marry you other than that I love you and I want to spend the rest of my life with you."

Wrapping her arms around my neck, she placed her forehead against mine. "I love you, Lucas."

I slipped my hand under her shirt where I expertly unclasped her bra. "I love you more."

It didn't take long before Hollie was stripped out of most of her clothes, and I had my pants off and kicked to the side.

She climbed onto my lap again and I pushed my fingers inside of her, both of us moaning.

"You're so wet," I said as I took her nipple into my mouth.

She dropped her head back and moaned. "I want you, Lucas. Now."

Pumping my fingers, I moved to her other breast. Hollie pulled her shirt off and then quickly pulled mine up and over my head, forcing me to break contact with her breasts.

I grabbed her and shifted until I was lying on the sofa with her on top of me. "I want to taste you."

Her cheeks turned red. "You want me to…"

With a wicked smile, I nodded. "Sit on my face and take your pleasure with my mouth."

Digging her teeth into her bottom lip, she crawled up my body and positioned herself over my face. I grabbed onto her hips and swore my cock had never felt so hard in my entire life. I reached down and took myself in my hand, pumping as Hollie began to grind herself onto my mouth and tongue.

It didn't take her long to bring herself pleasure as she rode my face. Each moan and whimper nearly caused me to come undone.

"Lucas!" she shouted. Her body trembled and I pumped my cock faster as she cried out, "I'm coming!"

And with those words, my own release spilled onto my stomach. Hollie moved off me and shifted so that she could lie down next to me on the sofa.

"That was amazing," she said softly, her finger tracing circles on my chest.

"Yes, it was."

She giggled. "I'm exhausted now."

Holding her closer to me, I whispered, "Close your eyes and rest."

Her breathing slowed while I felt her chest moving gently up and down. I found my own breathing begin to slow and it wasn't long before we were both sound asleep.

Chapter Seven

Hollie

The moment I'd mentioned getting married in Scotland, Lucas was on board. Since he still had some time before the dig site opened back up, we decided to head to Scotland for a week. I thought Ireland was beautiful, but Scotland was like a whole other world. It was beyond beautiful and a place I would for sure want to come back to and explore more of.

"We need to come back in the summer when it isn't so gloomy," I said as we walked hand in hand down one a street in Edinburgh. "We have to stay in the same place, though. The Dunstane is beautiful, and that little backyard courtyard is so adorable. I can't imagine what it's like in the spring and summer."

"It is a cute place. I think my favorite part is that copper tub."

I felt my cheeks heat. "We have had fun in it, haven't we?"

He nodded and laughed. "How did you find the hotel?"

"My friend Jemma, the one who lives in London, recommended it."

Lucas stopped walking and turned to face me. "You have a friend in London?"

I nodded. "Yeah. I met her years ago at a book signing."

Raising his brow, Lucas asked, "A book signing?"

"Yes, books," I said with a chuckle. "You know those things you open and read words out of? They transport you to another place and time and allow an escape? We were in the same online book club and found out we were both attending this huge signing in New York. We spent four days exploring New York City together and became fast friends. I visited her once in London a few years back."

"Wow, I didn't know that. Would you like to see her while you're here?" he asked.

"I've thought about it. Maybe once your time on the site is up, we can fly to London and stay for a few days before we fly home."

Lucas took my hand in his. "I would love that. I'd love to visit a few places while we're over here."

"That would be fun. Especially before we have the baby. I have a feeling our traveling days will be limited with a little one."

"I don't know, my parents didn't let kids stop them from traveling. I think we can still do it with the proper planning."

We walked for a bit longer before I said, "You know, we never did talk about kids. How many do you want?"

Lucas shrugged. "I never really thought about it. I don't know if I have a magic number. I guess it depends on what we both want. What we feel comfortable with. How about you?"

I looped my arm around his. "I'm like you. I never really thought about it. I'm not the least bit upset about the baby, but a part of me isn't too worried about having more kids. I guess I'm thinking like you. We just see how it goes."

He smiled as he looked down at me. I swore his eyes sparkled with happiness. "I like that plan. And if I haven't said it lately, thank you for being here, Hollie. I know what you gave up to join me in Ireland."

"I didn't give up anything, Lucas. I'm right where I want to be. I've been thinking, though. With the baby coming, I really think I want to be a stay-at-home mom. In our rush to start this relationship, we never really talked about money and all of that. My grandmother left me a trust fund. I don't really dip into it at all. If I did decide to sell my event planning business, I'd still have money to contribute."

Lucas took my hand and led me over to a bench where we both sat down. "First of all, you don't need to work if you don't want to. I make plenty of money working with the city to take care of our family. But if you want to keep working, I don't care either. The only thing I want is for you to be happy, Hollie. Money is just that...money. No matter what, we'll make do."

I squeezed his hand. "I love you for saying that. And love that you want me to be happy. I want the same for you. I should probably tell you that my grandmother was wealthy."

"Wait, which one?"

"My father's mother. She inherited it from her parents. They owned several businesses and he made most of his money from real-estate in New York and Boston. They left nearly all of it to me and Sarah. In a trust. I don't think Sarah has really touched hers and I only used some of mine to start my event planning business."

"Hollie, that's your money to do with as you wish. If you want to stay home with our baby, we'll be fine."

"It's *our* money now, Lucas. We're married and in this together."

We sat in a comfortable silence before Lucas exhaled.

"What are you thinking about?" I asked.

He shook his head slightly. "I was wondering what it would be like to live in Europe."

I chuckled. "Just think of all the ancient things you could dig up."

Smiling, he said, "I've had fun on this dig site and I'm glad I got the change to do it. But I've got to be honest, I miss home. I miss Salem."

"What are you saying?"

He stood and reached for my hand. "We have one more day in Scotland before the dig site opens back up. Let's not talk about work or the future or anything like that. I want to enjoy this last day in this beautiful city."

"I like the sound of that. What should we do now?"

Lucas waggled his brows. "There's a warm bed waiting back in our room."

I closed my eyes and said, "And a hot bath in that copper tub!"

The bell above the door rang out as I walked into O'Brien's. I took one glance around and froze in place. It was packed.

Lifting up onto my toes, I saw Kelley delivering some food to a table while another group attempted to get her attention. I wasn't sure what in the world came over me in that moment, but I rushed over to the table to help.

"What can I get for you?"

Four sets of eyes stared at me in utter shock. "You're American."

I placed my hand over my chest and said in a surprised voice, "What?"

"Who cares if she's American; I want another pint!" one of the men stated as he held up his empty glass.

Pointing to him, I winked. "One pint coming up. What else can I get you gents?"

The other three pointed to their empty glasses and one ordered a bowl of potato soup.

I quickly made my way over to the bar and then around it. "I need four pints!" I called out to a stunned Benny before I turned and headed into the kitchen.

Kelley looked exhausted while her mother, Sarah, whistled away as she dished up food.

"Sarah, I need a bowl of potato soup for one of the tables out there, please."

They both turned and looked at me.

"What are ya doing?" Kelley asked.

"I'm helping you. There's no way you can serve all those tables. I don't think I even saw one empty chair out there."

Leaning against the counter, Kelley wiped her brow. "There isn't any. The place has been packed since we opened! Once word got out that a director filmed a few movie scenes here, everyone has been trying to get in."

"I've never cooked so much in me life! It's a glorious day indeed!" Sarah called out as she handed food to Kelley who quickly put it on a tray.

"Are ya sure, Hollie?" Kelley said. "I could really use the help. I put a call in for me Cousin Lou, but she isn't here yet."

With a slight squeeze of her arm, I replied, "I'm sure. I waitressed in college. I've got this."

As Kelley walked out of the kitchen with her tray of food, I turned back to Sarah. She pointed her finger at me and said, "No lifting anything heavy, ya hear? A woman in your condition needs to be careful, no matter how well protected the wee one is."

I stared at her in stunned silence. Had I told her I was pregnant? Maybe Benny had. At any rate, I shrugged and smiled. "I promise to be careful."

"Here's the potato soup."

Apparently, I was moving too slowly because she yelled out, "Get a move on, girl! It's going to get cold."

Jumping into action, I put the bowl on the tray along with some sourdough bread. I'd eaten here enough to know what came with every dish.

The afternoon flew by, and I swore the steady stream of people didn't stop until around four. Once the pub was nearly empty, I sat down and put my feet up. Kelley did the same while Benny walked over and put a pint in front of her and a water in front of me.

"How do you do this every day?" I asked Kelley.

After taking a drink of her beer, she closed her eyes and let out a contented sigh. Focusing on me, she said, "I have never seen the pub that full. Not since I was a wee girl."

My eyes widened. "Seriously?"

At that moment, the door to the pub flew open, causing the little bell to protest, and a young girl around 20 years old came rushing in.

"I'm here!"

Everyone stared at her.

"You're a bit late, Lou," Kelley stated as she gave the poor girl the middle finger.

Lou looked around and only saw a few men sitting at the bar. I knew they were regulars since I saw them in the pub nearly every time I came in around this time. "There's no one here!"

"We were crowded at lunch time," Benny said. "Not an open chair to be found."

A wide smile spread over Lou's face. "That's good! Isn't it?"

"It's very good!" Benny replied.

"Wait." I sat up and turned to look fully at Benny. "What happened? How did everyone find out about the movie?"

Benny answered, "There was a write up in the paper about the pub being featured in a film. Guess folks were interested enough to come and check it out."

"Not just any paper," Kelley added. "But one that's available in all of Ireland. The author of the article mentioned how good me ma's cooking is and added in some history of the pub. They stated that it was in danger of closing if business didn't pick up."

I blinked a few times and asked, "Who was the author?"

Kelley and Benny both shrugged. "No idea," Benny replied. "But whoever it is, I owe them me thanks."

I felt myself smile.

The bell above the door rang once again and this time we all turned to see a very handsome, extremely well-dressed man standing there. He had on a dress coat that he took off and hung on one of the pegs before he made his way over to the bar.

"Nice to see ya again," Benny said as he greeted the guy. "What'll it be?"

The man pulled out a card, placed it on the table, and slid it over to Benny. Kelley sat up and leaned forward, causing me to do the same. Lou wasn't as discreet and made her way over to the back of the bar to look down at the card. Then she gasped.

"What?" I whispered as I turned to look at Kelley. "Who is he?"

"No clue," she replied in a hushed tone. "But by the look on me brother's face, he knows him."

Kelley and I got up and made our way around the bar, both of us attempting to look as if we were doing something else—though it was clear we were trying to listen.

"Mr. O'Rourke, it's an honor to meet ya, sir. Forgive me, I wasn't aware that was who ya were a few weeks back,"

Benny said as he reached across the bar and shook the guy's hand.

"That's okay. I don't expect everyone to know who I am."

Turning to Kelley, I asked, "Who is he?"

She blinked a few times then shook her head and focused on me. "He owns a brewery here in Ireland."

"He owns Guinness?"

Kelley rolled her eyes. "That's not the only beer! As a matter of fact, Mr. O'Rourke's pale ale was voted the best beer in Ireland last year."

"Really?" I said, turning back to the men. "What's he doing here?"

"I don't know," Kelley said softly.

"I'll cut right to the case, Mr. O'Brien," Mr. O'Rourke said. "I've been touring Ireland looking for a certain pub. I remember as a young lad, me da brought me to me very first pub to drink me very first pint. It was then I realized beer would become me passion. I couldn't remember the name of the pub, but I knew I would remember the moment I stepped into it. Old pubs like this tend to stay the same over the years. When I stepped into O'Brien's a few weeks back, I knew this was the place."

"I'm happy that our place was able to bring back good memories for ya," Benny said.

Mr. O'Rourke grinned. "I'm here for something more than memories, Mr. O'Brien. I'm launching a new beer, a stout. It'll be more on the sweeter end of the spectrum. Think of an iced mocha beer."

"That sounds delicious," Lou said with a wide smile.

"It is delicious," Mr. O'Rourke replied with a wink in Lou's direction. "I'm in the process of designing the label and coming up with the name. When I first tasted it, me mind was instantly transported back to this very pub. Your grandfather, I believe it was, brewed his own beer."

Benny nodded. "He did indeed. Once he died, me da stopped brewing. He said running the pub kept him busy enough."

Mr. O'Rourke nodded as if he understood. "It reminds me of that very first beer I ever had. Me da insisted I drink your grandfather's brew, when all I wanted was a Guinness."

Benny laughed. "It was me first taste as well, and it was that moment I knew I'd be running the pub after me da passed."

"I'd like to name the beer O'Brien's Stout, in honor of your pub and where I had my first drink. And to honor your grandfather as well. I'd also like to put a picture of the pub on the label. You'd be compensated, of course. If ya agree to it, I'd like to have the launch party here at your pub."

My heart pounded in my chest. I could only imagine how Benny felt. Sarah grabbed hold of my arm, and I was pretty sure she was holding her breath.

Mr. O'Rourke slid another piece of paper across the bar. "I believe the price is fair."

Benny's knees buckled as he read it and whispered, "I need to sit down."

Lou grabbed the piece of paper and then looked back at Mr. O'Rourke. "Is this for real?"

He nodded. "May we sit at a table and speak?" he asked Benny.

"Go to your office," Kelley stated. "Hollie and I can take care of things out here."

I nodded and smiled as I watched the two men walk toward Benny's office in the back. Once the door shut, Kelley rushed over and grabbed the piece of paper out of a stunned Lou's hands. She gasped and covered her mouth with her hand. Then she looked over at me, and I could see tears building in her eyes.

"Will it get the pub out of debt?" I asked, crossing my fingers behind my back.

"And then some," Sarah replied with a shaky voice. "This will pay off everything and leave a nice nest egg for Benny and Ma."

She walked over and showed me the amount on the piece of paper. It read one million. "Is that in euros or U.S. dollars?"

Both girls laughed. "It's in euros; it would be a little over a million in US dollars," Kelley said.

I pressed both hands to my mouth. "Are you serious?"

They both nodded and then they grabbed hands and started to jump around like schoolgirls. They quickly pulled me into the madness, and we all danced around together. I had never laughed so hard in my life.

"So this is a really good thing?" I asked.

"It's a blessed good fortune is what it is," Kelley said as she hugged me. "I think you're our lucky charm, Hollie Craft...I mean, Hollie Payton! Since ya walked through that door, Benny has had nothing but good fortune."

My cheeks heated. If she only knew. The last thing I could do was tell her why her brother was having such good fortune—if it truly was because of the spell.

Chapter Eight

Lucas

The second I walked through the door, Hollie ran up and threw herself into me. I wrapped my arms around her and laughed. "I think I like this welcome from my beautiful wife."

She drew back and I swore her eyes were lit up like the Fourth of July. "You're never going to believe what happened today!"

"Please don't tell me someone offered to pay Benny for some dick pics."

"What?" Hollie said, laughing. She shook her head. "No, no one asked him for any dick pics. I think you should sit down for this. Let me make you a drink!"

I watched as she rushed over to the kitchen and poured me a glass of champagne. Then she poured juice into another flute.

With a wide smile on her beautiful face, she made her way back over to me. "Thank you," I said as I took the drink from her.

"Let's sit down." Hollie pointed to the sofa.

After we sat down, she lifted her drink and I followed suit.

"To Benny getting an offer today that he couldn't refuse."

One of my brows rose. "What kind of offer?"

She nearly bounced off the sofa. "This well-dressed guy came into the bar who's about the same age as Benny. He said he owned a top brewery in Ireland and that his father had brought him to O'Brien's for his first beer when he was younger. It was such a great memory for him that he came back to visit a few weeks ago."

I tilted my head as I thought about the guy who'd been sitting at the bar, seemingly a bit out of place in his designer suit. "I wonder if it's the same guy I saw in the bar a few weeks back."

Waving my comment off, Hollie went on. "Anyway, he has a new stout beer coming out and he wants to name it O'Brien's Stout, and this is the best part!"

I waited as her grin grew bigger on her face, if that was at all possible. "What? What's the best part?"

"He wants to put a picture of O'Brien's on the label and do the launch party there and..."

I waited and motioned with my hands for her to spit it out.

Hollie brought her hand to her mouth then let it fall as she yelled out, "He's paying him a million euros for the use of the pub's name and photo!"

I blinked at Hollie for a few moments before I shook my head. "Did I hear you right? You said he's paying Benny a million euros?"

"Yes!" she cried out. "Kelley said it will pay off all their debts and that Benny will have a nice little nest egg left over for both him and their mother."

Placing her drink on the coffee table, Hollie took my hand in hers. "Lucas, it worked! The spell worked!"

My mouth fell open, and for a hot second I was about to dispute what she said, but then I clamped it shut.

Her smile faltered some. "You don't think it was the spell, do you?"

Squeezing her hand, I set my drink down next to hers. "I'll admit my first instinct was to say it was a coincidence, but with everything that's been happening to Benny, I think you're right. It has to be the spell."

"I called my Sarah today and told her what happened. She believes it was the spell as well. She said now that it's really happened, that should be it. No more weird offers of sex and feet pictures for money. Benny has fallen on his true windfall, and it was all because of my spell!"

I lifted her hand and kissed it. "Hollie, promise me one thing."

She beamed up at me. "Anything."

"You'll be more careful with the spells, especially since you're pregnant. The fact that our little one might be making your spells twice as powerful should be a warning."

She pushed her fingers through my hair as her eyes searched my face. When our gazes locked, she seemed suddenly serious. "I can't promise I won't do any spells."

"I'm not asking you to stop completely, I just want you to be careful with them."

"I promise you I'll be careful, and I won't do any spells without talking to you first."

"You mean that?"

She nodded. "Cross my heart," she whispered. Then she scrunched up her nose and added, "What if it's just a tiny little spell? Like the tiniest of ones."

I drew in a breath and gave her the look my mother used to give me when I was arguing some point to her.

"Fine, I won't do any spells without talking to you first. I do have one question, though."

"Give it to me."

"If our daughter or son has the gift, will you let me teach them how to use it?"

My head snapped back as I gave her what I was sure was a stunned expression. "Of course I will, why would you even ask that?"

With a one shoulder shrug, she replied, "I don't know. I know that my spells have gotten me into a bit of trouble here and there."

"Here and there?" I asked, trying not to smile.

Slapping me playfully on the arm, she giggled. "Yes, here and there. But I really wish my mother had spoken to me earlier when she saw the gifts I had. I might not have rebelled against the craft and learned to use my powers in more of... um...."

"An efficient way?"

"That's one way to put it. I don't want our child—if they have the gift—to feel lost like I did when I realized I had it."

I reached out and pulled her onto my lap. Wrapping my arms around her waist, I looked up at her. "You feel lost?"

"I did, at first. And terrified. When I put that hex on you, I was so upset. You were the last person I would ever want to hurt, but because I was messing around and not giving my gift the proper respect it deserved, I almost lost you. I don't want our child to ever feel that way."

I lifted my hand and tucked a piece of her brown hair behind her ear. "You didn't know at the time that it would have that impact on me. And I need you to know that however you want to raise our kids I'm behind you one hundred percent—whether they have the same gift as you or not."

I could feel the moment the tension left her body. "That means so much to me, Lucas. I love you."

"I love you too. Now, before we go over and congratulate Benny, I think I want to make love to my wife."

Her brows raised. "Really? I like the sound of that."

Lifting her shirt over her head, I quickly got to work taking her bra off. Because she was pregnant, her body was super sensitive to my touch. I took a nipple into my mouth and Hollie squirmed on my lap.

"Lucas, I need you. Now."

Letting her breast fall from my mouth, I looked into her desire-hazed eyes. "You don't have to tell me twice."

I had never seen the two of us move so quickly. We were undressed and back on the sofa in record time.

"I want on top," Hollie stated, pushing me down onto the sofa. When she crawled on top of me and slowly sank down on my dick, I thought I was going to explode then and there.

"That's it, take what's yours."

And take she did.

From the sound of people and music filtering out through the closed doors, there was clearly a celebration going on at O'Brien's.

"Sounds like a party," Hollie said with a chuckle.

"Sure does."

I pushed open the door and smiled when I saw a large crowd inside. In the back right corner was a small group of musicians, some old, some young. They were playing traditional Irish music while a few people danced in the middle of the pub.

"Let's see if there's a place at the bar!" I yelled to Hollie. She nodded and laughed while she took in the happy crowd. As we made our way up to the bar, Benny saw us and yelled for two young guys in their mid-20s to let us have their seats. They gladly got up and made their way over to a table where a small group of women sat.

"What a crowd tonight!" I shouted to Benny.

"It is! Word got out about the brewery. I'm sure your missus told you!"

Nodding, I helped Hollie slide up onto the stool as she yelled out, "Good news travels fast!"

"You're in Ireland, Hollie. Word moves fast in these parts!" Benny replied. "Pint?"

"Please!" I answered.

He looked at Hollie and she said, "Water, please!"

After placing my pint in front of me, Benny recapped what Hollie had already told me. I'd never seen him so happy. The stress lines between his eyes were gone and he had a light air about him.

"And I've got even more news," Benny stated.

"More good news?" I asked, glancing quickly at Hollie who simply shrugged.

"Casey and I are going to elope to Scotland, like ya and Hollie did."

I was positive my expression matched Hollie's. Shocked.

"When?" Hollie asked, or rather shouted.

"When things die down a bit here at the pub. Things will be moving quickly with the new stout launch. There's a photographer coming tomorrow to take pictures of the pub and some other big shot from the brewery who wants to take a look at the place. They're going to start planning the launch party right away. I do hope you'll both still be here when it happens. I mentioned to Mr. O'Rourke that ya do party planning, Hollie. I hope ya don't mind."

"I don't mind at all!" Hollie said with excitement. "I'm so happy for you, Benny. It couldn't have happened to a better person."

His cheeks turned a slight shade of pink.

"And it's all due to ya, Hollie," a voice said from my left. Turning, I saw Sarah standing there. She handed me a bowl of Irish stew before placing another one in front of Hollie, who seemed stunned into silence.

"Ma's right," Benny said. "You've been like a good luck charm ever since ya stepped foot in the pub."

Hollie relaxed and laughed. "Nah, it's all just a coincidence."

Someone down the bar called out for Benny. He tapped the bar in front of us and then quickly made his way toward them. Sarah was still looking at Hollie with a strange expression.

"Is everything okay, Sarah?" Hollie asked.

Reaching across the bar, Sarah took Hollie's hand. "When I was a wee girl, me ma told me about her best friend who liked to collect herbs and flowers from the forests. She would make potions and medicine for the town folk. One time, I watched when she did this dance in the middle of the forest. I asked her what she was doing, and she said she was giving thanks to the sun and moon for her gift. Most folks said she was a witch, a good one. Not the kind who dally in the dark arts, but the kind in touch with mother nature. It was a gift."

Hollie sat there frozen as she stared at Sarah. "You have the same gift; I see it in your eyes. It wasn't a coincidence that me Benny's luck changed simply from ya popping up. Ya helped him."

"Sarah, I…" Hollie's voice faded. She wasn't about to lie, nor would she deny her gifts.

With a wink, Sarah patted Hollie's hand. "Be mindful of the wee one you're carrying. She'll make your gift stronger."

My mouth fell open. "You know about that?"

Sarah turned back to me and winked once again before she headed back to the kitchen. Hollie and I both looked at one another and then started to laugh.

"Do you think she always knew?" I asked.

Hollie shrugged. "I have no idea. She never made it seem like she knew."

We were still laughing when Benny walked back up. "What's so funny?"

Turning to look at him, we started to laugh even harder.

Chapter Nine

Hollie

If there's one thing you can say about the Irish, it's that they know how to throw a party. O'Brien's had a steady stream of people coming and going for the two-day celebration of the launch of O'Brien's Stout. The first day had been the official launch party with the media and top executives from the brewery in attendance. It was fun, but the crowd at the party today—with more hometown folks, family, friends, and Mr. O'Rourke in attendance—was a rowdier bunch. I had never laughed so hard nor had so much fun.

"Do you need any help?" I asked Lou as she rushed by with a tray full of beer.

"No! Ya have fun and enjoy the party."

Mr. O'Rourke walked up to me with a smile on his face. "I want to thank ya, Hollie, for taking the reins and planning the launch parties."

Only a few days after the deal had been signed, Mr. O'Rourke had called to offer me the job of planning both launch parties. I had to admit, it had been a blast and not the normal type of events I was used to planning. But while I was planning the events, it had made me realize that I didn't miss my job back home. Party planning used to be my passion, but after everything that had happened between me and Lucas, my newfound craft, and being pregnant, I found that I longed for a simpler life. A small part of me wanted to stay in Europe and raise our first born in Scotland. But then I quickly realized I would miss my family far too much to do that.

"It's been my pleasure," I replied as I shook his hand.

"Ya know, if you're looking for a job while you're in Ireland, we could use someone like ya on our team at the brewery."

For a moment, I was stunned into silence. "Wow. My goodness, that is such an honor, and I can't thank you enough for the offer, but I think I'm going to focus on one job right now," I said as I patted the small bump that wasn't really visible yet.

His eyes drifted down then quickly back up to meet my gaze. "Congratulations to ya and Lucas."

Smiling, I replied, "Thank you so much."

"Will ya be here in Ireland long enough to have the baby?"

I quickly peeked over at Lucas before I focused back on Mr. O'Rourke. "I'm not sure. This dig is proving to be a rather big one. The weather keeps putting a halt to things, though only for a day or two at the most. I think we'll know more in the next few weeks. It would be kind of fun to have the baby here, though."

"Kelley told me ya got married in Scotland?"

"That's right!" I said, searching the pub for Kelley. It hadn't been lost on me how much time Mr. O'Rourke had been spending with Benny's sister. And they both seemed to look for one another when they walked into a room. "It was a last-minute decision and one I'm so glad we made."

He gave me a polite smile.

"How about you, Mr. O'Rourke, are you married or dating anyone?"

"Please call me David, and no to both."

My heart did a weird little excited skip. "Really? Then you're single and ready to mingle?"

His brows drew in for a moment, and then he laughed. "I guess ya could say that."

Kelley walked by and David followed her with his eyes until she disappeared into the crowd.

"Are you heading back to Dublin this evening?" I causally asked.

Snapping his attention back to me, he gave a small smile. "Kelley offered to let me stay in her guest bedroom."

I had to bite in my cheek to keep from smiling. "That was sweet of her. She's so amazing, especially with how she helps Benny and Sarah run the pub."

He grinned. "I agree. Benny speaks very highly of his sister, as he should. We've spent some time together, and she truly is amazing."

I couldn't help but smile. "She certainly is. Any guy would be lucky to call her his."

David nodded but kept his mouth clamped shut, so I kept talking.

"Since I've known her, she's spent most of her time here at the pub. I don't think she's dating anyone. As a matter of fact, I know she's not. I mean, not that you were asking."

David's brows shot up in surprise before he smiled. "Right."

"Nope, pretty sure she's single."

"And ready to mingle?" he asked on a laugh.

"Yes!" I said, laughing as well.

A feeling of warmth filled my body, and I knew it was because Lucas had walked up behind me.

"What's going on here?" Lucas asked, giving me a kiss on the cheek and a head nod in David's direction.

"Hollie was informing me of how dedicated Kelley is to the pub," David answered, a twinkle in his eye.

With a smile of my own, I replied, "I was doing just that."

"Did I hear you mention something about her being single?" Lucas asked, a warning tone in his voice.

"Did I?" My voice was dripping with innocence.

"Ya did." David cleared his throat and added, "I should mingle around."

"Of course!" I said, nearly pushing him away from us. "Go and enjoy yourself."

David looked at Lucas and nodded before he turned his attention back to me. "It was a pleasure talking to ya, Hollie."

"The pleasure was all mine."

Once David was out of earshot, Lucas took my elbow and led us toward Benny's office. As soon as we were inside, he shut the door and ran his hand down his face. "Hollie, you promised me you'd stay out of other people's business, and now you're clearly trying to set David and Kelley up."

I held up my finger as I said, "No, I promised I wouldn't do any spells without talking to you first. I wasn't doing any spells."

"But you were thinking about it."

I blinked at him a few times before I asked, "How did you know that?"

He stared at me with a disbelieving look on his face. "Because I know you! It's like I can sense when you're thinking about doing magick. It's weird because that feeling is growing stronger and stronger."

I pressed my hands to my mouth to cover a gasp.

"What?" he asked.

"What if you...what if you're...oh my God!"

"Hollie, what is the matter with you?"

I swallowed the words I was dying to yell out, but I knew I needed to talk to my sister Sarah before I said anything to Lucas.

"I think it's simply because you're getting to know me better and better. I'm sure that happens with all couples."

He nodded. "Probably. I am learning to read you more."

"You're right, though, I was thinking about how easy it would be to put a little spell on David and Kelley, but I'm not going to."

He raised a single brow. "You're not?"

I slowly shook my head. "I'm not, I promise you. I'm going to let it play out the old-fashioned way."

Lucas smiled. "Good, I'm glad. If it's meant to be then it will happen."

"But," I said as I held up a finger again, "that doesn't mean I can't give a little nudge here and there...the old-fashioned way."

Drawing in a deep breath, Lucas sighed heavily and rubbed at the back of his neck. "Why do I feel nervous about that statement?"

With a wide grin, I replied, "There's absolutely nothing to be nervous about. Nothing at all!"

There was a light knock on the door and Lucas reached behind him to open it. Kelley stood in the doorway looking worried. "I saw ya walk back here; I hope I'm not interrupting."

"Not at all!" I replied.

"Do ya mind if I speak to ya, Hollie?" Kelley asked. My eyes instantly went to where she was rubbing her hands together nervously.

"Is everything okay?" I asked.

"To just Hollie?" Lucas asked at the same time.

Turning to look at him, I asked, "Why did you ask it like that? Why wouldn't Kelley want to talk to me?"

"I don't know, I guess I was surprised is all."

"Why?" Kelley and I asked in unison.

Throwing up his hands, Lucas shook his head and turned to leave. "I will never understand women."

And with that, he walked out of the office, shutting the door behind him.

Focusing back on Kelley, I asked, "What's up?"

She chewed on her bottom lip before she blurted out, "I think I'm attracted to David."

Nearly jumping with pure happiness, I reached for her hands. I had forgotten what life was like before the use of magick. The feeling you got when something happened the good old-fashioned way. Then again, maybe it was a different kind of magic. Smiling, I replied, "That's wonderful!"

Looking confused, she asked, "It is?"

"Yes! I think he's attracted to you too. I mean, he keeps looking at you."

She huffed. "That doesn't mean anything. He's a man, they look."

"That may be, but he was *looking* at you."

"Does that mean something different in America?"

I laughed. "He likes you, I know he does. Call it intuition."

Her eyes lit up and filled with curiosity at the same time. With a slight tilt of her head, she asked, "Is it because you're a witch? Is that how ya know he likes me?" She gasped. "Oh my gosh, are ya able to read minds? Me ma said she knew a woman once who could read the minds of others. Not all the time, but she could tell things about people that no one else could. She would always say it was intuition. That's why ya said that, because you're a witch."

"Wait. What?" I asked in a voice so shrill I could have broken glass. "What do you mean because I'm a witch?"

She waved me off. "Please, me ma had ya pegged from day one. Plus, there's no way me brother would be approached by all those women and offers on his own. Don't get me wrong, he's a nice-looking lad, but please!"

Kelley laughed while I chewed on my thumbnail.

When she finally stopped laughing, her face grew serious. "Will ya help me like ya helped Benny?"

I took a step away from her and the only thing that came out of my mouth was, "What?"

"A spell! Can ya put a spell on David?"

With a quick shake of my head, I replied, "You can't use magick like that. I can't make anyone fall in love with you."

"Oh, I don't want him to fall in love with me. I simply want him to notice me."

"You don't need me for that, Kelley, I'm telling you. He likes you. He...he...he told me he did!"

Another gasp slipped free from her mouth. "He did!"

Turning away from her, I replied, "Yes." Then in a lower voice I added, "Kind of."

I closed my eyes and counted to ten before I faced Kelley once again. "You don't need my help, I promise you. I've tried this before, helping a relationship with a little push."

"And did it work?"

Screwing up my face, I tried to think of a way to explain that it worked by not working. "I don't know how to answer that. Considering I nearly killed Lucas and caused my best friend's love interest to start stalking her, I'm going to say no."

Kelley's eyes went wide. "Right. Let's not go with any spells to help then."

Pointing at her, I replied, "Smart move. My best advice is to keep it simple and be yourself. If David likes you, which I'm almost a hundred percent positive he does, it will be because of you, not some spell."

I hadn't been ready for Kelley to launch herself into my body and I nearly stubbled back.

"Thank ya so much, Hollie!" Pushing me back at arm's length, she smiled at me. "I don't know how ya do it."

"Do what?" I asked.

She gave me a knowing look. "I think you know!"

Before I could respond, she rushed past me, opened the office door, and rushed out.

I exhaled as I closed the door. I knew it was the middle of the night for my sister Sarah, but I pulled out my phone and hit her number anyway. She answered after four rings.

"It better be good, Hollie, or I swear I'll fly on my broomstick to Ireland and throat punch you."

Leaning against the office door, I ignored her and said, "Sarah, what's the likelihood that Lucas could...you know... be...one of us?"

It only took her a minute to burst out laughing. When I didn't respond, she sobered up. "Oh my gosh, wait, are you being serious right now?"

Nodding, I let out a breath and said, "Totally serious. I think Lucas is a witch."

Sarah was silent on the other end before she finally whispered, "She was right."

To be continued in *A Bit of Razzle Dazzle,*
releasing summer 2023.

Other Books by Kelly Elliott

Stand Alones

The Journey Home*
Who We Were*
The Playbook*
Made for You*
*Available on audiobook

Boggy Creek Valley Series

The Butterfly Effect*
Playing with Words*
She's the One*
Surrender to Me*
Hearts in Motion*
Looking for You*
Surprise Novella TBD
*Available on audiobook

Meet Me in Montana Series

Never Enough*
Always Enough*
Good Enough*
Strong Enough*
*Available on audiobook

Southern Bride Series

Love at First Sight*
Delicate Promises*
Divided Interests*
Lucky in Love*
Feels Like Home *
Take Me Away*
Fool for You*
Fated Hearts*
*Available on audiobook

Cowboys and Angels Series

*Lost Love**

*Love Profound**

*Tempting Love**

*Love Again**

*Blind Love**

*This Love**

*Reckless Love**

*Available on audiobook

Boston Love Series

Searching for Harmony

Fighting for Love

*Series available on audiobook

Austin Singles Series

Seduce Me

Entice Me

Adore Me

*Series available on audiobook

Wanted Series

*Wanted**

*Saved**

*Faithful**

Believe

*Cherished**

*A Forever Love**

The Wanted Short Stories

All They Wanted

*Available on audiobook

Love Wanted in Texas Series

Spin-off series to the WANTED Series

Without You

Saving You

Holding You

Finding You

Chasing You

Loving You

Entire series available on audiobook

*Please note *Loving You* combines the last book of the Broken and Love Wanted in Texas series.

Broken Series

*Broken**

*Broken Dreams**

*Broken Promises**

Broken Love

*Available on audiobook

The Journey of Love Series

Unconditional Love

Undeniable Love

Unforgettable Love

*Entire series available on audiobook

With Me Series

Stay With Me

Only With Me

*Series available on audiobook

Speed Series
Ignite
Adrenaline
*Series available on audiobook or coming to audiobook
soon

COLLABORATIONS
Predestined Hearts (co-written with Kristin Mayer)*
Play Me (co-written with Kristin Mayer)*
*Dangerous Temptations (*co-written with Kristin Mayer*
*Available on audiobook

www.ingramcontent.com/pod-product-compliance
Lightning Source LLC
Chambersburg PA
CBHW071238170626
46809CB00015BA/3068